D0890091

THE AMERICAN REVOLUTION

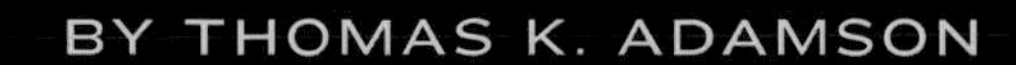

BY THOMAS K. ADAMSON

Published by The Child's World®
1980 Lookout Drive • Mankato, MN 56003-1705
800-599-READ • www.childsworld.com

ACKNOWLEDGMENTS
The Child's World®: Mary Berendes, Publishing Director
Red Line Editorial: Editorial direction
The Design Lab: Design
Amnet: Production
Content Consultant: Robert J. Allison, Chair, History, Suffolk University

Photographs ©: Corbis, cover, 18; National Atlas of the United States, 5; Bettmann/Corbis, 6, 12, 23; Tarker/Corbis, 9; Library of Congress, 10, 15, 16, 19, 21, 29; The Gallery Collection/Corbis, 11; North Wind Picture Archives/AP Images, 22; Steven Wynn/Thinkstock, 25; Photos.com/Thinkstock, 27

Design Element: Shutterstock Images

ISBN 9781631437076
LCCN 2014945397

Printed in the United States of America
Mankato, MN
November, 2014
PA02243

ABOUT THE AUTHOR

Thomas K. Adamson has written dozens of nonfiction books for kids on sports, space, history, math, and more. He lives in Sioux Falls, South Dakota, with his wife and two sons. He enjoys sports, card games, and reading and playing ball with his sons.

TABLE OF CONTENTS

THE BATTLE OF BUNKER HILL

Peter Brown marched with a few hundred other **patriot** soldiers. They stopped on a hill near Boston. These soldiers were fighting for the right of the 13 **colonies** to govern themselves. On June 16, 1775, they spent all night building trenches and walls. In the morning, Brown and his fellow soldiers saw British warships gathering in the harbor.

Early in the morning the warships fired at the patriot army. An exhausted Brown kept building dirt walls. He heard nonstop explosions from the cannons. Brown worked faster.

British soldiers formed long lines. The colonists called the British soldiers redcoats. The redcoats began marching up the hill. Brown and his fellow fighters fired

49°
(to Massachusetts)
New Hampshire
Massachusetts
New York
Rhode Island
Connecticut
Pennsylvania
New Jersey
Maryland
Delaware
Virginia
North Carolina
South Carolina
Georgia
MAP KEY
★ ★ ★
The 13 Colonies
Native American reserve
Spanish territory

Though the redcoats eventually won the battle, heavy casualties shook their confidence.

their **muskets**. They held the British back. The British had scouted the hill the day before. Nothing was there. But Brown and the other colonists had built a defense overnight. The strong defense surprised the British. Another line of soldiers advanced up the hill. The crack of muskets seemed unending. Brown saw some of his fellow soldiers run away from the battle. But he meant to stay and fight.

The British eventually gained the top of the hill. Brown saw many of his fellow soldiers shot. British soldiers stabbed others with **bayonets**. Patriot officers ordered their soldiers to retreat. Brown retreated with the rest of the surviving fighters.

The Battle of Bunker Hill was a victory for the British, but they suffered heavy losses. The powerful British were surprised at how hard the patriots fought. It was the beginning of what would be a long war.

The British had to march uphill into gunfire to get to the patriots. What do you think it was like to march toward soldiers pointing guns at you, knowing you or your friends might be shot?

TAXES, PROTESTS, AND BOYCOTTS

★ ★ ★

In the 1700s, Great Britain ruled its 13 colonies in North America from all the way across the Atlantic Ocean.

Britain and France fought over territory in North America. They both wanted to control more area. They fought a war for seven years. Both Britain and France had Native American allies. The British called it the French and Indian War. It lasted from 1756 to 1763. Britain won the war. But the war cost the country a lot of money.

Britain left an army in the colonies for their protection. The British made the colonies pay for this army through taxes.

The taxes angered the colonists. They didn't want to pay for things they didn't get to vote on. The colonists called it

Bostonians threw snowballs, sticks, and stones at the redcoats before the British began to fire.

taxation without representation. To protest, the colonists started a **boycott** of British goods. They refused to buy anything that came from Britain.

Some protests in Massachusetts turned violent. British soldiers killed five people in Boston. People in the colonies heard about the event. They began calling it the Boston Massacre. The colonists' frustration with the British grew.

King George III

In 1773, colonists were angry about a tax that had been placed on tea. On December 16, one group boarded a ship loaded with tea. They showed their feelings about the tax by dumping the tea into Boston Harbor. This protest became known as the Boston Tea Party.

King George III of Great Britain closed Boston's port. No supplies could get to the colonists in the city.

In the fall of 1774, all of the colonies except Georgia sent leaders to Philadelphia. This meeting was called the First Continental Congress.

COLONIAL COMMUNICATION

In the 1700s, there were no phones or radios. It took more than a month for a letter to cross the ocean. Britain did not close the port of Boston until June 15, 1774, more than five months after the Boston Tea Party.

It was the first time that leaders of the colonies got together. The leaders stated their loyalty

Colonists upset by British taxes dressed up as Native Americans and threw tea belonging to the British East India Company into Boston Harbor on December 16, 1773.

Minutemen fought the redcoats at Lexington, the first real battle of the war.

to Britain and King George III. But they also argued against Britain's right to tax them. They agreed to form an army. They would stop all trade with Britain.

The British governor of Massachusetts, Thomas Gage, decided to capture the colonists' supplies of ammunition. On the night of April 18, 1775, he sent 700 redcoats to Concord, Massachusetts. On the way, the British soldiers met a group of patriot soldiers at Lexington, Massachusetts. These volunteer soldiers were called minutemen because they could be ready to fight "at a minute's warning."

The two groups faced each other for a few quiet moments. Then someone fired a shot. No one knows who fired that first shot. Both sides began firing. The colonists scattered. The British moved on to Concord.

More patriots were waiting at Concord. They fired at the redcoats and forced them to run back to Boston. They attacked the retreating British soldiers from the woods and from behind fences. The revolution was now a real war.

Some colonists supported British rule and were called loyalists. The colonists who supported independence were called patriots. Some thought the patriots were traitors. What would you do or say if someone called you a traitor for doing what you thought was right?

WAR BREAKS OUT

★ ★ ★

In June, hundreds of minutemen from New England marched to Boston. They fortified a position on Breed's Hill.

In the early morning of June 17, 1775, the British fired their cannons. The patriots did not move. The British then marched up the hill, planning to attack up close. To save ammunition, the colonists waited to fire until the British were close. The first wave of British fell back. Many of them were killed. But the British had more soldiers and more weapons. Another line advanced.

The British reached the top of the hill. They attacked with bayonets. The patriots did not have bayonets. They could only swing their muskets in defense. Finally, the patriots retreated. The British took over the hill, winning the bloodiest battle of the war. More than 1,000 British soldiers were either killed or wounded. The patriots lost just over 400.

Minutemen were able to respond quickly to British threats. ►

A famous line from the Declaration of Independence reads, "We hold these truths to be self-evident, that all men are created equal, that they are endowed by their Creator with certain unalienable Rights, that among these are Life, Liberty and the pursuit of Happiness."

The patriots' fierce fighting surprised the British. This battle showed that the war was not likely to end quickly.

Even after these battles, most colonists were not interested in complete independence. This changed when they heard that King George wanted to crush the rebels. More colonists began to favor independence.

Colonial leaders worked on declaring themselves an independent country. A carefully written **declaration** would persuade others to support the cause for independence. It could also convince other countries to support them. The Declaration of Independence was approved on July 4, 1776.

The British now planned to attack New York City. They hoped to control the Hudson River. Doing this would divide the colonies in half.

Congress had formed the Continental Army. They sent George Washington to command it. Washington prepared his men for battle. He knew his troops had little experience in war. In late summer 1776, Washington and his army moved in to defend New York. The British sent in 15,000 soldiers. The British landed on Long Island on August 22.

Some redcoats marched around the main patriot line. They attacked from behind. The patriots fought well but had to retreat. Almost the entire patriot army was trapped between the British army and the East River.

COMMON SENSE

In January 1776, Thomas Paine published a pamphlet called *Common Sense*. Paine argued that the colonists did not need a king. Paine's plain way of writing made sense to many colonists. He convinced many of them to support independence.

Patriot soldiers from Delaware fired their muskets during the Battle of Long Island.

The British stopped their attack. The British commanders still hoped to convince Washington to end the rebellion. Instead, Washington and his men took boats across the river to Manhattan. A heavy fog hid Washington's troops from the British. The British did not realize the patriot army was gone until the next day.

Washington's army was outnumbered. The men were not well trained for battle. Washington decided to avoid large battles. He had his army make small attacks and quick retreats.

Washington's army moved across New Jersey. In December 1776, the British and German soldiers called Hessians moved within miles of Philadelphia, where the colonial leaders met. The British had hired the Hessians to help them in the war.

George Washington

Washington's army crossed the Delaware River into Pennsylvania on December 7, 1776. The army camped there for the winter. The British were unable to attack any further in the cold weather. Most of the British soldiers went back to New York and spent the winter in comfort. The Hessians stayed on the New Jersey side of the river.

Many of Washington's men deserted, or left the army without permission. Some went home to tend crops. Others were not prepared for the harsh life of a soldier. Washington worked hard to persuade the men to stay and fight. He also sometimes had soldiers whipped for disobedience. If you were leading reluctant troops, which strategy would you use? Why?

BATTLES

Washington's army was now down to approximately 6,000 soldiers. The British had them on the run. **Morale** was low. Washington desperately needed a victory. He planned a risky surprise attack.

On Christmas night, Washington and his army crossed the Delaware River. Chunks of ice floated in the river. Snow and wind blew around the patriots. The surprise worked. The attack on the Hessians in Trenton ended with more than 100 Hessians killed or wounded and almost 1,000 taken prisoner.

On January 3, 1777, Washington's army marched to Princeton. The patriots rushed forward right at the British. They won a furious battle. The British soldiers who were not shot ran away.

These successes gave the colonists hope to go on. Many new volunteers signed up to join the fight.

In late August, the British landed in Maryland and moved north toward Philadelphia. Washington lined up his army along Brandywine Creek.

On September 11, the British marched in line right at them. They crossed the creek and captured several cannons. Washington's army fought for hours. Then it had to retreat. The British took over Philadelphia on September 26.

Another part of the British army attacked the colonies from Canada. The British army had to cross difficult terrain. The patriots slowed the British by chopping down trees across

Washington led his troops across the Delaware on December 25, 1776.

The British defeated the patriots at the Brandywine, but they failed to destroy Washington's army.

their path. The British moved less than one mile (1.6 km) per day. They ran out of supplies. The British stole food from local people's homes, which made more people support the revolution.

CAMP FOLLOWERS

Many citizens helped the patriot army. They carried supplies, did laundry, and helped the sick and wounded. Many were soldiers' wives. Others simply wanted to help the cause. Still others made a living this way. The army needed these camp followers for its survival and success.

The patriot army prepared for battle at Saratoga on October 7. The British were shocked that they were outnumbered. The patriots defeated the British on October 17. They had now won a major battle.

The colonists were finally ready to believe they could truly be free from the British. The French also believed the patriots could win.

France was ready to get back at the British after losing the French and Indian War. In February 1778, France agreed to support the revolution.

While the patriots beat the British at Saratoga, Washington's army of 11,000 men arrived at Valley Forge to spend the winter. The army was tired and cold and had few supplies. It was a difficult time. But at Valley Forge, Washington's army learned how to march and fight better. In the spring, the improved army was ready for action.

On June 18, 1778, the British left Philadelphia. They went back to New York. Washington's army left Valley Forge to follow them.

Washington's army endured a harsh winter at Valley Forge.

On June 28, the two sides battled near Monmouth Courthouse, New Jersey. The battle ended in a draw. Washington's army rested for the night. By morning, the British were gone. They arrived in New York by early July.

The British were getting nowhere in the north. They decided to invade the southern colonies. There were more loyalists there. The British also thought the slaves in the south would rise up against their slave owners.

In late November 1778, the British invaded Savannah, Georgia. The patriots fled, greatly outnumbered. The British then moved north and took Charleston, South Carolina.

Washington made Nathanael Greene a new commander of southern armies. Greene went to North Carolina in late November. The soldiers had little clothing and no food. The soldiers stole food from farmers and townspeople. They had lost the will to fight.

Greene knew the army could not win large battles. It carried out small attacks against the British where it could. He got the army fresh supplies while it stayed constantly on the move. Greene made the British chase them around for months. The British ran low on supplies.

When the armies went through a town, many townspeople feared for their safety. Many left their homes.

The British stole from the vacant houses.

Greene's army then prepared to fight at Guilford Courthouse, North Carolina. Greene's men fought hard but could not hold their ground. The army retreated.

In the South, the British won many battles but not the war. Not as many loyalists joined the British as they hoped. And the French were now on their way to help the patriots.

Nathanael Greene

Slaves had virtually no rights in the colonies. Still, many were able to choose to fight in the Revolution. Both sides offered freedom for slaves who joined their army. Do you think a chance at freedom would be worth the risk of fighting in a war?

PEACE AND INDEPENDENCE

In August 1781, Washington learned that 29 French ships were on their way to Chesapeake Bay. He also knew that the British were setting up at Yorktown, Virginia, which had access to Chesapeake Bay. Washington and French commander Jean-Baptiste de Rochambeau hurried to Yorktown with 16,000 troops.

The French blocked Chesapeake Bay. No supplies could arrive to help British general Charles Cornwallis. Cornwallis was one of Great Britain's most talented generals. He had won several battles in the war. French and patriot soldiers then surrounded the British at Yorktown.

General Cornwallis surrendered to Washington following the Siege of Yorktown.

The colonists and the French gradually moved cannons forward as they defeated the British outer defenses. They closed in on Cornwallis's army.

Washington and Rochambeau's men blasted the British with cannon fire day and night. On October 14, Washington sent in the soldiers to attack. They forced their way through the British defenses. The patriots yelled, "Rush on, boys! The fort's ours!"

Cornwallis was left with no choice. On the morning of October 17, a British officer appeared with a white flag. This meant that the British wanted to surrender. Cornwallis had seen that his situation was hopeless.

The Treaty of Paris officially ended the war on September 3, 1783. In the treaty, the British had to admit that the United States was a free and independent country. The treaty set the American borders. It also allowed British forces like the one in New York to leave. By the end of that year, the British were gone.

How did the patriot volunteer soldiers defeat the largest professional army in the world? Most patriot soldiers had never been in war. But they fought bravely. General Washington made some brilliant moves and daring plans. The help that France provided made victory possible.

After the Battle of New York, Washington's plan changed from trying to win the war to simply not losing. This plan eventually wore down the British army.

THE CONSTITUTION

There were many challenges after the war. The national government was weak. The states operated like separate countries. The new country needed a stronger central government. In 1787, delegates met to write a Constitution. This document defines Americans' rights and how the government should be set up.

Washington led his victorious army into New York City on November 25, 1783, the day the last British troops left the colonies.

The British were also surprised at how hard it was to defeat the patriots. The British did not think the colonists could keep fighting for so long.

The patriots were also fighting for a cause they believed in. This difference might have been the one that mattered the most.

Loyalists liked their way of life under British rule and did not want it to change. What do you think it was like to be a loyalist in America after the British lost the war?

TIMELINE

March 5, 1770	Redcoats kill five people in the Boston Massacre.
December 16, 1773	Colonists dump British tea into Boston Harbor.
April 19, 1775	The first battles of the war take place at Lexington and Concord.
June 17, 1775	The British and patriots clash at the Battle of Bunker Hill.
January 1776	Thomas Paine publishes *Common Sense*.
July 4, 1776	Colonial leaders approve the Declaration of Independence.
August 1776	The British win the Battle of Long Island.
December 25, 1776	Washington crosses the Delaware River and launches a surprise attack in Trenton, New Jersey.
Winter 1777–78	Washington's men spend the winter at Valley Forge.
June 1778	The Battle of Monmouth ends in a draw.
March 15, 1781	Greene's army fights the British at Guilford Courthouse.
October 1781	The patriots surround Yorktown.
October 17, 1781	Cornwallis surrenders following the siege of Yorktown.
September 3, 1783	The Treaty of Paris ends the Revolutionary War.

GLOSSARY

bayonets (BAY-uh-nets) Bayonets are long blades that can be fastened to the end of a rifle and used as weapons. Both sides used bayonets in the Revolutionary War.

boycott (BOI-kaht) A boycott is when people refuse to do business with someone as a protest. The colonists' boycott of British goods helped lead to the war.

colonies (KAH-luh-neez) Colonies are lands that have been settled by people from another country. People from Great Britain settled 13 colonies along the East Coast of North America.

declaration (dek-luh-RAY-shuhn) A declaration is a formal announcement. American leaders wrote a declaration that said they were an independent country.

deserted (di-ZUR-tid) Soldiers who deserted ran away from the army. Some soldiers deserted rather than face the war's harsh conditions.

loyalists (LOI-uh-lists) Americans who sided with the British during the Revolutionary War were called loyalists. The British thought more loyalists would help them fight the patriots.

morale (muh-RAL) The spirit or mood of a person or group is its morale. Leaders try to keep their soldiers' morale up so they will fight better.

muskets (MUHS-kit) Muskets are a type of long gun. Muskets were used by soldiers in the American Revolution.

patriots (PAY-tree-uhts) Patriots were Americans who were in favor of independence from Britain during the Revolutionary War. Patriots joined militias or helped the war effort in whatever ways they could.

traitors (TRAY-turz) People who help the enemies of a country are traitors. Some called the patriots traitors for fighting against the British.

TO LEARN MORE

BOOKS

Aloian, Molly. *George Washington: Hero of the American Revolution*. New York: Crabtree Publishing, 2013.

Carson, Mary Kay. *Did It All Start with a Snowball Fight?: And Other Questions about the American Revolution*. New York: Sterling, 2012.

Cheatham, Mark. *Life of a Colonial Soldier*. New York: PowerKids Press, 2014.

WEB SITES

Visit our Web site for links about the American Revolution: **childsworld.com/links**

Note to Parents, Teachers, and Librarians: We routinely verify our Web links to make sure they are safe and active sites. So encourage your readers to check them out!

INDEX